This Journal Belongs To

Norbert

Virginia K. Freyermuth

I moved to a BIG city.

NORBERT

What Can Little Me Do?

With lots of help from

Julie Freyermuth and

Virginia K. Freyermuth, Ph.D.

POLLY PARKER PRESS LLC®

That night I wondered,
what can little 3-pound me do in this BIG new city?

Momma said, "Norbert, let's go for a walk and find things to do."

I wished I could woof
like the LOUD collie dog,
but my mini mouth
makes a very mini sound.

I can't do what big dogs do.
What can little me do?

I wished I could give rides
like the BIG STRONG horse,
but my little legs are too short
and too weak.
I can't do what horses do.

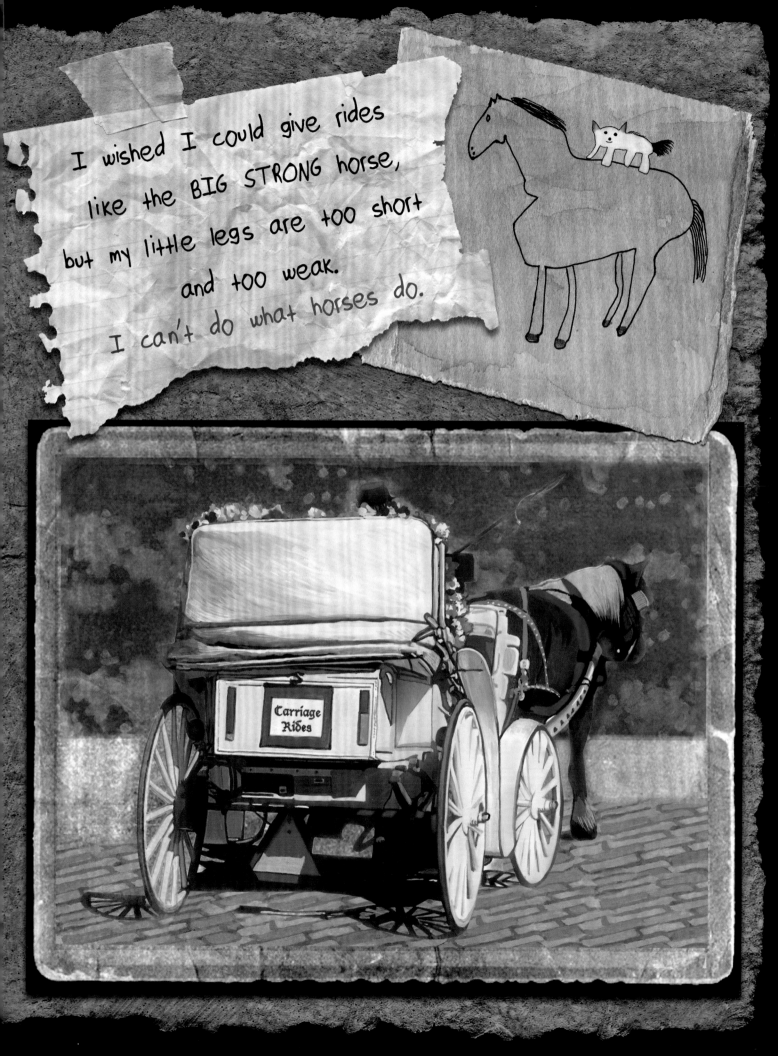

We went back to the park.
Kids yelled, "Look! Look! What is that?"

I wished I could fly in the sky like the birds,
but I have no wings, so my paws stayed put.
I can't do what birds do.
WHAT can little me DO ?

I wished I could swim like the ducks on the pond,

but my furry body's not made for wet places.
I don't even like baths!

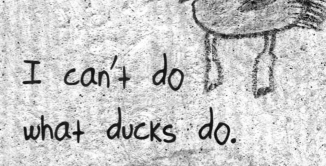

I can't do
what ducks do.

What can
little me DO?

 I wished I could climb up a tree like the squirrel,

but I fell on my belly and felt pretty silly.

I can't do what squirrels do. What CAN little ME do?

☀ The Next Day

Momma said,
"Let's take the subway
and go to the store."

Everyone had
somewhere to go,
something to do.

Except me.

I couldn't even climb the stairs,
'cause every step was way too high.

I can't do what big dogs do.
I can't do what horses do.
I can't do what birds do.
I can't do what ducks do.
I can't do what squirrels do.

WHAT CAN LITTLE ME DO?

Nothing.

At the store,
the sales lady said,
"You're the littlest
dog I have _ever_
seen. You must
make everybody
SMILE!"

Momma said,
"That's what my little Norbert does best."

He makes people SMILE
just by being himself!

Then I realized, THAT'S what I can do!
I can make people smile.
(And that was always true).

Right from the start
making people smile
was my greatest gift.
I only had to follow
my very BIG heart!

The sales lady told us we should become a Registered Therapy Animal Team. That's just what we did, and we now volunteer to bring smiles and comfort to many in need.

Pet Partners
Touching Lives, Improving Health

ABOUT LITTLE ME

Date of Birth: March 27th

Nicknames: Norbie, Norbs

Dog Breed: Mixed

Full-grown Height: 7" tall

About Pet Partners®

"Pet Partners' Therapy Animal Program trains volunteers and evaluates volunteers with their pets so they can visit patients/clients in hospitals, nursing homes, hospice and physical therapy centers, schools, libraries and many other facilities."
www.petpartners.org

I have an awesome badge and everything! Our volunteer work brings joy, comfort, and of course, smiles to lots of people.

MY FAVORITE STUFF

To Do: Walk in the park, Take naps, Play with stinky socks, MAKE PEOPLE SMILE

TO EAT: Turkey, Chicken, Eggie-schmeggie, kibble

TOYS: Froggie, Blue Monkey, Stinky Socks, striped ball

TRICKS: High Five, Zen (lie down)

Dedicated to Harry, Hannah, David, and Sarah

Special thanks to JEFFREY C. FREYERMUTH for creating Norbert's handwriting and pencil drawings.

Many thanks to Richard Freyermuth for his support and encouragement.

Polly Parker Press, LLC is a mother-daughter-owned and operated independent children's book publishing company.

Copyright © 2013 Polly Parker Press, LLC

First Edition

Polly Parker Press, LLC
P.O. Box 34
South Carver, MA 02366
info@PollyParkerPress.com
www.PollyParkerPress.com

Publisher's Cataloging-in-Publication Data

Freyermuth, Julie.
   Norbert : what can little me do? / Julie Freyermuth [and]
Virginia K. Freyermuth.
      p. cm.
   ISBN: 978-0-9848682-0-9 (hardcover)
      1. Dogs—Fiction.   2. Self-actualization (Psychology)—
Juvenile fiction. 3. Picture books for children.   I.
Freyermuth, Virginia K. II. Title.
PZ7.F892 No 2013
[Fic]—dc23

                                        2013910596

Printed in China

1 0 9 8 7 6 5 4 3 2 1

The illustrations in Norbert's Artist's Journal were created with traditional and non-traditional mixed media. Some of those materials include:

handmade paper
tea-stained paper
paste paper
watercolor paper
antique paper
recycled paper
fabric
watercolor
tempera paint
gouache
acrylic
ink
marker
pencil
crayon
pastel
colored pencil
masking tape
glue stick
scanned doodads & digital stuff
Jeff's handwriting & pencil drawings for Norbert
--*pretty much everything but the kitchen sink...*
Wait! Norbert takes baths there. Does that count?

What can YOU do?

For information on how to create a Norbert Artist's Journal, and to see fun photos of Norbert, visit his website at:

www.norbert.me